To Robin

Moss on Stone

SANDRA WILLIAMS

Thank You for your work and inspiration.

Sandra

ISBN-13:978-0692739938

BOOK & COVER DESIGN: Sandra Williams

ILLUSTRATIONS: Robert Louis Williams

γνῶθι σεαυτὸν

SONO PUBLICATIONS

ROCKPORT, MASSACHUSETTS

AUTHOR'S INTRODUCTION

Moss on Stone was inspired by Susannah Norwood Torrey (1826~1908), who lived in Rockport, MA, and is based on the diary she kept as a young woman (March 1848~August 1849). She speaks to us who live in a very different time, but not so different in experience. All times are times of change. All lives are fraught with the joys and sorrows of being human.

Here is the story of Susannah's particular joys and sorrows, beautifully expressed in her diary entries, enlarged upon and imagined through fiction. The story is told from her perspective in an afterlife as she reviews and reflects upon the span of time recorded in her diary—with the insights and knowledge acquired over her lifetime and beyond.

Susannah's vibrant, thoughtful and creative individuality shines through her diary entries, so much so that relegating her only to brief mention in a historical record, or to a chance find of her diary was not an option for the author.

~⁓

NOTE: Entries from Susannah's diary and from Solomon Torrey's letters to Susannah are italicized, but not dated, as the narrative does not consistently follow chronology, but rather thematic subjects throughout. Multiple entries separated by asterisks indicate a span of days. Throughout the text, words, phrases and/or sentences from the diary and letters are italicized within quotation marks. Susannah's diary entries have been edited by the author only for consistency and clarity.

Let us go forth, the tellers of tales, and seize whatever prey the heart longs for, and have no fear. Everything exists, everything is true, and the earth is only a little dust under our feet.

W.B. YEATS, *THE CELTIC TWILIGHT: FAERIE AND FOLKLORE*

Twas thus I heard the dreamer say,
And bade her clear her clouded brow;
For thou and I, since childhood's day,
Have walked in such a dream till now.

Watch we in calmness, as they rise,
The changes of that rapid dream,
And note its lessons, till our eyes
Shall open in the morning beam.

AN EXCERPT FROM "A DREAM"
WILLIAM CULLEN BRYANT (1794-1878)

DEDICATION TO MY FAMILY

"But if the while I think on thee....
All losses are restored and sorrows end."

PROLOGUE

To have a dream is to remain hopeful—a vision of some future time when all will be well and worry ceases. I found that when dreams fade there are other ways, if not to cherish thoughts of the future or to reflect upon regrets of the past, then to sustain us day to day with a small measure of light. Mine were things of beauty—moss on stone.

Now, from this distance of space and time—those earthly illusions that do not exist here—I linger, preparing to return to life anew. What did I leave behind? A portrait for others to look upon, a scrapbook of moss designs, a diary, and a stone cottage by the sea.

I review my life as one would a colorful tableau, with the insights and knowledge that come when the physical body is no more. I see mine was a life worth living. I will tell you something of that life: of dreams and dreams fading, of intimations and transformations, of time passing, of dear family and friends loved and lost, and of people and places changed.

Through it all, were the immutable gifts of nature to renew my soul with unequaled joy, asking nothing in return.

Between this thicket and the wood, lay the sought for valley covered with rocks piled one about another without a spot of ground large enough to set my foot for near an acre, and these rocks were covered with the most beautiful mosses that I ever saw.

I
Paradise

It resembled more a fairy picture than a thing of reality.

I was Susannah Norwood Torrey. I was born, lived my life and died on a small enclave narrowly separated from the mainland by the lovely Annisquam River: Cape Ann, with its myriad inlets and quiet, hidden coves all along its rocky coast.

The first explorer to visit Cape Ann was Samuel de Champlain in 1605. As a child I heard stories of his coming ashore at what we called Whale Cove. There he was met by Indians who welcomed him to a foreign shore. They danced for him and drew a map of the coastline. The first white man known to set foot on the Island Cape (as he named it), Champlain thought it remarkable, "…covered with trees of different sorts…. quantities of vines on which the unripe grapes were a little larger than peas, and also many nut trees…." and surrounded by the three islands we knew as Straitsmouth, Milk, and Thacher.

Then came John Smith in 1614. He dubbed our fair isle "Tragabigzanda," after a Turkish princess, as the story went. The three surrounding islands he called the "Three Turks' Heads." He too was impressed and inspired by the cape's beauty and worth. He rightly foresaw that, "Here every man may be master and owner of his owne labour and land....If he have nothing but his hands, he may...by industries quickly grow rich."

Later, Charles I of England renamed our island Cape Ann in honor of his mother Queen Anne.

Cape Ann, reaching out into the Atlantic, was desirable to explorers and immigrants alike for its natural beauty; access to the open sea; and its abundant fish, timber and granite.

And so, seafaring souls—immigrants all—set sail for a new life and the safe harbor of "le beau port."

Among them, Francis Norwood, my great, great, great grandfather sailed from Gloucestershire, England with only his dreams and hopes for a prosperous future dependent on an untamed land, the vast sea and the labor of his own hands.

It was not long before schooners sailed in from and headed out to ports all over the world. The settlers became lobstermen, fishermen, farmers and stone cutters —gathering in catches from the shallows and the deep, working to transform rocky soil into farm and grazing land, and quarrying the earth for its windfall harvest of granite.

Francis Norwood received a six-acre land grant, as did other settlers, with a stipulation to build a house within a given time. The house he built still stands proudly along Goose Cove, then a remote settlement. He and his wife Elizabeth not only survived, but thrived to establish generations of Norwoods on Cape Ann.

O, what courage, fortitude and endurance they must have had to create a life for themselves, and for those generations to come!

I was a fifth generation Norwood. I grew up in the comfort and ease of what by that time was a large and prominent family whose legacy is to have helped shape the history and vibrant life of Cape Ann. The Norwoods started businesses, expanded land holdings and built cottages and houses extending from Goose Cove to Pigeon Cove, to Straitsmouth and along Sandy Bay. Some were modest, some stately. My husband Solomon and I built our house in Rockport in 1850—our "kingdom by the sea."

It was in the shape of a dream.

During my lifetime, summer visitors and artists were the latest travelers to discover Cape Ann. My uncle, William, opened a boarding house in Pigeon Cove, one of the first of that novel trade on the island, serving varied company. Then, and subsequently, many visitors came and still do—the famous and the obscure—wishing to experience the peace and beauty found there. Ralph Waldo Emerson, Henry David Thoreau, and William Cullen Bryant, a few of the more prominent among them, frequented our once hidden jewel.

They all would have agreed, as did my ancestors (and as residents and visitors have since), that John Smith's words were true: Cape Ann is, "the paradise of all those parts that I have seen....I would rather live here than anywhere."

Cape Ann underwent many changes during my lifetime. In 1840, our town of Rockport was incorporated. The railroad expanded from Boston to include Cape Ann, at Gloucester—long since a thriving fishing and trading port. Very quickly the railroad connection resulted in an even busier Cape Ann. Yes, many and ongoing were the changes—some were welcomed; some were not. Some were dramatic, some hardly noticed.

Not so with the vicissitudes of nature—always changing, yet somehow constant, always welcomed and ever an inspiration to those who observe—no matter the season.

II

SEASONS & SPINDRIFT

*Nature's book is ever open showing a thousand beauties
to delight and interest, but how many walk this
Earth and heed it not.*

John Quincy Adams had just been laid to rest when I
began to keep a diary in March of 1848. I thought of
it as a *"receptacle for daily events, and also a chronicle
of pleasant memories wherein after years, when old age
creeps in on pace, I may look upon with heartfelt
pleasure."* And I did turn to it many a time in those
"after years" to recall with pleasure, and sometimes
with sorrow, what was put down within its cover.

In youth, can one ever imagine how life's
changes may defer or help realize a wish, a hope, a
dream?

As children, on so many afternoons, I and my
dear sisters Ora and Aria went along the beaches and
coves. We wandered off into the shadowy forests or
sunny meadows, walking and playing among boulders,
which we thought grew out of the earth. We saw in
their various formations, castles, caves for creatures, or
pedestals for angels. Later, I came to feel those great

monoliths as dark and solid sentinels—counterbalance to the watery expanse of the sparkling sea.

Then summers were endless as we roamed under blue skies and brilliant sun. On cold or gloomy days, time passed slowly indoors by the hearth fire with the sound of rain on the roof, or the wild wind whining against the door. In more pleasant weather, we rode in carriages to visit neighbors and friends, took picnics to a favorite cove, or fished off Sandy Bay at sunset.

My sisters and I loved to be in the gardens, planting and weeding, then collecting the seasonal flowers, fruits and vegetables. In late summer and early fall, we worked with our mother and grandmother to put up the harvest for the cold months ahead. And so, I grew with the pleasure of play and the purpose of work, in the light and love of family amid the natural beauty of our island which blessed us with its many gifts for the senses, soul, and spirit.

How could I not have become aware of all that surrounded me, or not feel myself to be part of it? I became a keen, somewhat romantic observer and lover of nature's varying palettes. Each season created its own mood and magic—dabbled upon canvases of earth, sea and sky.

Although at first I was apt to become rather nostalgic as the appeal of one season faded into the next, the emerging one quickly persuaded me to revel in and welcome *its* unique bounties.

March had parted with many tears, and the winds are sighing its requiem.

Ah! Spring: with carpets of crocuses.

I was awakened this morning by the song of the first robin. How many pleasing thoughts that voice suggested—the return of spring, with its birds, sunshine, showers and soft breezes....It is a lovely morning and spring seems returning in good earnest, though probably before old winter gives up his reign

*to his more lenient successor, he will give a few more
parting tokens of his authority.*

The mercurial nature of the weather between
seasons has the power to take us unawares, causing
dramatic shifts, not only in weather, but in mind and
mood as well.

*Great was my surprise this morning to see it
snowing quite fast, and upon looking from the window,
the earth, which but yesterday was quite green, with all
the surrounding objects was covered with snow. A dreary
spectacle indeed after such fine weather, and my thoughts
caught the spirit of the outward gloom, which has
haunted me during the day.*

The briskness of fall: the commotion of color, the
dry whisper of swirling leaves—calls to awaken me from
summer's sleepy spell.

*Autumn...with her bountiful gifts to reward the
husbandman for his labors. Beneath her touch, the fields
wax yellow with the ripening corn, and orchards rich
with fruit. She breathes through the forests, and they
blush with a thousand beauties that languid summer
never dreamed....The sun pours down its milder rays,
and the bracing winds impart a buoyancy to the step and
spirits. All hail, October!*

And always—the sky of infinite wonder above:

*Not until after the extinguished light last evening
did I notice the beautiful appearance of the heavens,—
there was the least bit of a moon visible and the
stars were uncommonly bright,—the sky had a dark
leaden hue forming a striking contrast with the
beautiful Northern Lights, which were remarkably
bright, and their reflections gave to the landscape
and ocean beneath a most lovely appearance. The
winds were still; the ocean was calm, with a few
white sails scattered here and there over its
peaceful bosom.*

I learned much from nature—watching and
listening as I quietly went about the fields, shores and
woods—until I was apt to see myself reflected in its
varied forms and hues. The natural transformations
all around were familiar, yet each season brought
surprising reminders of the abundance and loveliness
of change to the earth and to the world within me.

All there was to be seen and appreciated under
another's gaze might have been experienced as
ordinary, but I saw the sublime.

From my soul perspective now, I see that my
world was small, but warm and bright. My mind was
wide, and my life full of grace and many blessings—

not the least of which was living at the land's edge beside the fickle sea.

The sea lived in me—even formed me: to inhale its salty air; to hear its many voices, roaring or quietly lapping the shore; to see its stormy swells, or cloudy sea smoke along the horizon. In dark times, I heard wave after wave as a lament, or felt it an omen when fog rolled in off Sandy Bay cloaking our town in a grey mist.

In all of its aspects, the sea had the power to move me, and was a faithful companion from cradle to grave.

A most beautiful walk by the seashore of my old ocean home, I cannot but love it—not only for being my native place, but for its variety of wild and majestic scenery, the ocean extending further than the eyes can reach, with a few islands scattered here and there along its rock girt coast. Its hills and well-cultivated valleys— its big woods and almost endless variety of natural curiosities—among which is the Whale Spout and Gully, which I have visited today, the latter caused by the water being pressed through an aperture in the rock at a particular time of the tide. By the pressure from beneath, the water is thrown up several feet. The Gully with [its] unpoetical name will soon be mentioned with the things that were. During a storm last year, the outer end was broken away by the force of the waves, and a large piece of stone weighing fifty tons was precipitated into the lower end that was open to the seas.

I cherished those days of roaming without a care, of discovery in solitude, as I did the nearness of my dear family and friends—the former offering quiet wonder, the latter consolation and affection.

While I anticipated and welcomed nature's changes and surprises, I did not take well to change in my own life and avoided it if I could, especially when it involved the absence or loss of loved ones.

The more I observed and experienced in nature, the more I felt the world around me and the world within me were ever weaving a pattern—but one not quite discernible—until now.

III

LOVE & LOSS

O, we have been happy, very, very happy.
I could have born most anything but this parting.

Once, when just 17 years old, I sat for a portrait which
my dear friend, Mrs. Sarah Allen, had persuaded me to
do—such was her impish charm. I had learned from her
that Mr. Alfred J. Wiggin, a painter later well known for
his portraiture, admired me and wanted to paint my
portrait. For amusement, I agreed to sit for him, and I do
believe he managed to capture something of my
melancholic nature, as well as a hint of mystery (which I
was to myself back then).

More than once, the point was made by Mrs.
Allen that Mr. Wiggin thought me beautiful and wished
to pursue a courtship, had I been willing. Although the
thought of it "*excited my vanity*," I was *not* willing—not
in the least!

It was on a lovely autumnal afternoon that Mr.
Allen and wife, and Mr. Alfred Wiggin called for me to go
with them to collect moss. We went in Norwoods pasture
and found an abundance. After collecting a sufficiency,
Mr. Allen proposed going down to the spot by the
seashore to see a pyramid that Mr. Wiggin and himself

*had worked all the day before to build....It was very
pretty and about six feet high and twelve in diameter.
We were all very gay, and while the gentlemen were
pitching quoits, Mrs. Allen and myself sat by the
water's edge casting pebbles and watching for the
seventh wave, as she mentioned that one of the poets
said, "And the seventh wave outstrips them all."
When about to return, she sang to us the beautiful
words of "The Slave Mother." We left this spot and
went up as far as Norwoods Head, and whilst looking
down into the water from its almost perpendicular
heights, she play-fully remarked that it would be a
very romantic story were I to fall from its heights into
the yawning gulf below and Mr. Wiggin should rescue
me and then we fall in love and marry each other.*

We laughed at her conjured scenario. Unlike
many young women, I did not dwell upon thoughts
of romantic encounters, courtship or marriage. Though
I knew marriage was expected of me, and that one day
I would marry, Mr. Wiggin could never have been my
intended husband. I found him, "*very conceited and
exceedingly credulous; nothing was too marvelous for
him to believe.*"

After that day, Mr. Wiggin came several times
to call on me. On one of those visits, he brought a
friend with him, a Mr. Solomon F. Torrey, who had seen

my portrait and wanted to meet me. When Solomon was introduced to me, he said I was even lovelier than portrayed, at which I believe Mr. Wiggin shifted back and forth in a nervous manner. Mr. Torrey had seen my portrait, but I had never seen him. When I did set eyes on him, it may have been *I* who was imagining a romantic scenario, not so different from the one Mrs. Allen had invented on our outing.

Solomon was tall and slim with hair the color of sand. I thought he had a regal countenance, with a rather piercing gaze from very blue eyes, like the look of the ocean at noon on a cloudless day.

It seemed Solomon and I were like minded. We spoke of the weather, of course—a much expected topic of conversation on Cape Ann—then of music, of books and of our interests. He told me of his work as a stone cutter in his father's quarries in Rockport and Quincy. I spoke of my family and of my love of mosses. I showed him an album of botanical specimens I had collected and dried. He said it was well done.

Mr. Wiggin must have felt quite overlooked, as I recall feeling that Mr. Torrey and I were the only persons present in the sitting room for the rest of the afternoon, such was the mutual attraction.

We found much in common and seemed compatible in every way. I was surprised and a bit apprehensive at the intensity of our engagement that day. I daresay, we were more than pleased to have been introduced. We began a courtship shortly thereafter, of which both of our families approved.

Mr. Wiggin soon began to see how matters stood and never called but a few times after, but tried in every way to set Solomon at variance with me.

Solomon and I later admitted to each other that after our first meeting we somehow knew our destiny together was sealed.

And so, I married my love Solomon. We were young, and our hearts longed for a family and our own home. Thereafter, his singular effort was to secure for us an independent future, for we lived with my maternal grandparents, right next door to my childhood home, where my parents lived, on Mt. Pleasant Street in our little town of Rockport.

Solomon worked long hours in his family's business, which often took him to Boston. On those days he arrived home quite late. We looked forward to the evenings, no matter the hour. It was our time together to dream about the future. Father had reserved a plot of land for us along Sandy Bay where we would one day make our home. In our evening conversations, we began to plan for our life there. What could it be? What shape would our dream take?

Solomon endlessly made drawings of the possibilities, each so unique—very different from any other house in our whole town. He made sketches of each room, and together we made designs for a beautiful iron gate to welcome family and friends.

We often walked down to the plot to imagine where our home would be built, outlining different areas with stones where the foundation might be until we decided how it would be best situated for sun and wind and for a view of the harbor. In the following months and years we continued to plan. We began putting in gardens and planting trees—longing for the time when we would see our stone cottage rise up out of its foundation. There we would grow old together.

Before we were struck with unimaginable loss and separated by time and distance, life was full and good.

Two years after we married, we welcomed a beautiful son, William Francis. Although we joyfully anticipated his birth, we never could have conceived of what enveloped us the moment we held him for the first time and saw perfection. When we looked into William's eyes, he grasped our fingers as infants do. It was clear he would be dependent upon us to ensure his future health and well being. We silently acquiesced to be there for him ever after.

A light had come into our lives—so brilliant it was nearly unbearable. Solomon and I spoke of the nature of this feeling, previously unknown and entirely unimaginable to us before William's arrival. It was a tender ache, inspiring the wish and intention to protect the purity of the mind, body and soul entrusted to us.

Solomon and I realized our own parents must have had similar thoughts and feelings for us at our births. A circle was closed, connecting our families in wonder and the welcomed obligations of parents. This heavenly enterprise we embarked upon with both solemnity and great lightness of being.

Family and friends alike were drawn to William, a most pleasant and playful boy he was—fine boned and pale, like Solomon. His hair was light and grew into curls around his face. His eyes were dark like mine, and they were bright and shining. He was a spirited child, but tender as an infant, and with a joyful soul.

I remarked to Solomon, "William will be lively and restless like his father."

He agreed and added, "I don't think he will be as fond of solitude as his mother," but he believed William would have my sensibilities and practical nature.

Even in the brief time he was with us, we had plans well into the future for his boyhood, his schooling, and even spoke of grandchildren he might one day present to us. Such is the future-bearing inspiration of children and the vast scope of dreaming parents.

William grew so quickly. Before long we found ourselves walking behind him, holding on to his little hands, as he put one tiny foot in front of the other with a smile of accomplishment on his face. Soon he would be walking on his own.

We had planned a family gathering in honor of William's first birthday. Grandmother promised to make fried chickens, a family favorite, and Mother would bake fruit pies. I made a white cotton suit with blue embroidered smocking for William to wear on his day.

Then, on a morning just before his first birthday, the golden light that he was grew dim. As was his habit, Solomon went to fetch William to bring him to us in the morning, but found him very warm, flushed and crying softly. We could not comfort him and called for my grandparents. Soon, my parents and Aria also arrived, and we sent for the physician. He attended to William and said he appeared quite ill, but he believed the malady would soon pass. He left us with remedies and instructions for poultices to administer through the night.

Surely his vitality would return before long, and we would see our boy's precious smile once more.

That was not to be.

Baby William died in my arms a few days later. Despite our fervent prayers and infinite hope, there was nothing to be done. I was left to wonder if I had only dreamed it all—dreamed that William had been with us, engendering such depth of commitment and purpose.

To the end of my life I could not recall with any clarity the following hours and days. Again and again I asked myself, "What will I do with the ocean of love remaining with no place to flow to on this earth?" All that was left to us were bittersweet memories of the source and dearest object of our affections, a few toys, a daguerrotype of our darling, and a small plot of ground marked by a granite headstone, though visits to it became fewer and far between as the months passed.

It was too hard.

Solomon and I had each other, and at least, from time to time took momentary solace in our mutual loss and grief. There is promised comfort in those supposed words of wisdom, "Time heals all wounds." I once had thought them to be true, but with the loss of William, scars remained, and ever after out of the blue, pain returned just as deeply and fully felt as at the moment of loss.

IV

SOLITUDE & SOLICITUDE

A visit to the forest and then, my little captive,
you are free.

Some say opposites attract, but Solomon and I had much in common. We had the same aims for our future. We treasured our time together and were devoted to our families, wishing to be of help to them whenever needed. Our deepest bond was the shared love and sorrow for our lost child.

We did, however, have very different temperaments. His nature was sanguine, restless as the wind; his sense of adventure was broad and grand. Unlike his, my nature was earthbound, settled, melancholic and contemplative. Solomon was more content in society than I. We both longed for and sought adventure, but each in our own way and in very different places.

He was curious—interested in history, maps, exploration and expeditions. My interests were quiet, small in circumference, but infinite in creative spirit and pleasure, solitary, and two in number.

Both of my "adventures" required being apart from daily life and routine. One was in the quiet reflection upon my thoughts, feelings and experiences. The other was in nature, indulging in my greatest pleasure—my especial love of mosses. It may be hard for you to imagine the thrill I felt when moments were found to steal away to my garret—alone.

The morning spent in solitude....a source of much pleasure, as well as profit, by way of affording me time for uninterrupted reflection, and also for giving the imagination the reins to build a few air-castles occasionally.

On the evenings when the hours stretched away waiting for Solomon's return, I listened for the familiar approach of the stage coach from Gloucester. Removed from the day's cares and chores, I was free to think or to write in my diary. I recorded in a line or two the mundane happenings of a day; the greater portion I devoted to descriptions of *my* "expeditions" into nature or to musings about my moods and memories.

Once alone, I might simply have closed my eyes to recall the liberation only to be known when standing at edge of the ocean with its vast view toward the horizon, or of the seclusion in field or forest. Often, I would sit at a window where there were delights to be enjoyed any time of the year—gentle breezes off the bay, the scent of lilacs in spring, the shower of gold as the ginkgo tree let down its leaves in fall, or snowflakes drifting like feathers gently down to the earth below.

A most lovely evening, and while seated at Ora's window, I noticed a beautiful appearance of a sloop, as she slowly turned in the cove, her white sails bending to the breeze, and moved gracefully out upon the moonlit waves....I heard the frogs sing for the first time this season and my heart leaped joyfully at this additional token of returning spring.

Time did not exist when setting out to discover an exquisite sea moss of muted mauve or deep red; the infinite varieties of dense ground moss of golden hue or vibrant green; or the thin layers of clinging moss—seemingly painted on stone.

Always a joy to me—the appearance of moss; the smell of it, briny or earthy; the feel of it—slippery or velvety—enchantment! Then there were the many lovely and lilting grasses—spiky or feathery in wood and meadow. A double delight it was to find the perfect specimen, then upon returning home, to create a pleasing moss design on pasteboard or to weave a basket or grass mat—heavenly.

I learned from Mr. Allen the manner of preparing sea moss and today went down to the shore to collect some. I brought them home, put them in water to select the most beautiful specimens. These I again immersed in water with the paper, upon which I carefully laid out the little branches with a needle. In removing it from the water, I was well pleased. It resembled the finest and most delicate painting, the rich colors contrasting beautifully with the white of the paper, but still success is not certain until they are pressed and dried.

I wished to share the allure of my discoveries through arranging them into pleasing designs. Was it my way of capturing beauty in time? Perhaps—yes, to be admired or contemplated by others at some future date. A Grecian urn captured a moment in time and once inspired Mr. Keats to write an ode to it:

When old age shall this generation waste
Thou shalt remain, in midst of other woe
Than ours, a friend to man, to whom thou say'st,
"Beauty is truth, truth beauty,—that is all
Ye know on earth, and all ye need to know.

It was thrilling to think that just beyond the ridge, over the next hill, or washed ashore at low tide, there were treasures to receive with reverence and gratitude. I accorded them pride of place in my scrapbooks,which I left behind, hoping they would be passed on for other generations to see and to appreciate —the beauty and the truth of them.

Frequently, I set out to a spot I had identified as yielding certain types of moss. Better yet was to come upon a hidden glen or narrow, pebbled beach where I might spy moss of a certain shape and color waiting for me alone. My heart raced in absolute exhilaration.

Far out of the sight of any habitation...the wind drew through the trees shaking the dry leaves,— making the solitude seem more solitary. Ever and anon a heavy gust would come and cause me to start and look about me, but fear did not take away the pleasure of my walk, for I love a little daring.

Under the spell of nature I was lost to myself. It felt as if I somehow *became* the sunny meadow or the tree branches soaring above it all. It happened more than once though that a movement or a sound would suddenly bring me back to myself, and the separation was always startling.

I took the winding road leading to the woods. The way was covered with a soft green carpet with tall trees on either side whose branches met here and there in hazy arches above me. After walking a considerable distance and becoming fatigued, I sat down upon a moss covered stone to contemplate this lovely scene. The cool breezes drew through the thick pines where sunlight seldom strays stirring the lighter forest leaves and fanning my burning cheeks as it passed along. The birds skipped and

*chirped amid the branches above me filling the air
with music. But suddenly there came one discordant
note to break the harmony, and I was awakened to the
loneliness of my position by the voice of a crow as it
flew from a dry branch just above me. I arose with fear
and trembling and turned suddenly to retrace my steps.*

Although I never travelled far or visited other
lands—I was transported through my senses—all of
them open among the rocks, trees, fields and sands—
gazing at the blue heavens, feeling the warm earth
under my feet, hearing the tall trees sway and the sad
cry of the wood thrush. All seemed to merge into an
awareness of a presence—a Spirit in nature, which
being sublime had the power to lift me to a place that
was not a place—rather like this realm of waiting.

These were my adventures—not far, but
"wider than the sky."

Another adventure, though without any hint
of the super-sensible, was a feeling of communion
with other souls, which launched me on excursions
of the mind and heart. My solicitude toward certain
intriguing and admirable souls was a powerful force.
I had often wished I could meet them face to face to
express my admiration and to ask the many questions
that arose in me. Such feelings, inspired by hearing or

reading about people and events—whether near or far, stirred both my imagination and my empathy.

Yesterday, George Gray the hermit...aged 78 died at his home in Lynn where he has been living in loneliness for about fifty years. His early history is shrouded in mystery, as he ever evaded questioning upon the subject. He was a very eccentric but worthy man, and also well educated, and capable of imparting knowledge of most of the higher branches, though the mechanical arts most engrossed his more particular attentions. He ever went about very thinly clad, often wearing old shoes without stockings, and garments besides being spare and ragged—not scrupulously neat, though not from inability to procure better, as he left a property of three or four thousand dollars. He has often been known to walk to Boston to attend literary and scientific lectures on winter evenings and back again—a distance of twenty miles clad in this manner with a dilapidated straw hat that had seen the snows of many a winter. I believe he was quite a poet. He left a valuable library which was sold at auction for two-,or three-hundred dollars.

Then, there was the well-known, local legend of Heartbreak Hill in Ipswich, a nearby town. The tragic name, the story was told, had originated in the fate of parted lovers. An Indian maiden kept watch on a hill over the waters awaiting her sea captain's return which, alas, was never to be.

One evening I learned a more sobering account of how the name "Heartbreak Hill" came about. On our way home after working in our gardens, Solomon and I stopped in below to see Grandmother. Soon after, *"The family kept dropping in one after another until we were quite a party,"* so we stayed on for tea and conversation. Someone mentioned a Dr. Manning, who had purchased Heartbreak Hill, a lifetime dream of his. Though his dream had come true only days before his death.

The topic aroused my curiosity about the associations with the tragic lovers, and I asked Grandmother about it.

It was a sad story. Here was made the last effort of the red man to regain their rights. Here they were defeated and left the battle field with broken hearts and fortunes. They called a solemn council and determined to gather the remains of their tribe, [and] *leave the homes of their fathers and their inheritance forever and travel towards the setting sun. At intervals of a few years, a company of Indians, the remnants of a once noble race, make a pilgrimage to this spot to visit the graves of their fathers and to think in sorrow over the downfall of their once mighty people.*

Grandmother set me straight with the true story, though nonetheless tragic than the one usually given out and believed by many.

I also had a great interest in events abroad. It was disheartening to hear of the injustices and inhumanity of the powerful against the helpless.

By the arrival of the Caledonia, *we have accounts of the revolution in France, and the flight of Louis Philippe, probably the last King of the French, together with the Royal Family, and Guisot and their safe arrival in England....And last, but not least, the* Moniteur *publishes another decree as follows—Slavery is to be abolished at once in all the colonies of the Republic! In this have they preceded us—and may the day not be far distant when slavery, that foul blot upon <u>our</u> Nation's glory, be struck out. <u>Then</u> may we <u>truly</u> sing of freedom.*

It was heartening to learn of certain individuals' courageous and selfless efforts on behalf of peoples desiring freedom, no matter where in the world the plight. Those brave and noble souls who devoted their lives to liberty for the common man gave hope that good may someday triumph over evil. One such soul was Louis Kossuth, governor of Hungary, whose efforts and travels I followed as I was able.

The affairs from Europe are of deepest interest.
The struggle of freedom with tyranny. There is still
hope for Hungary though opposed by Russian and
Austrian legions....Their all is at stake. They are
fighting for their homes and firesides, and their leaders
are noble and brave....I am enraptured with Kossuth,
the gifted and patriotic Hungarian leader. There is no
living character for whom I feel a deeper reverence.
He seems just the man for the hour.

The state of Massachusetts invited Mr. Kossuth
to visit and speak at the State House and many other
places throughout New England. At each of his
appearances he was welcomed by throngs. At Fanueil
Hall in Boston he made his last appearance and
speech, where he was likewise greeted. His message,
which I later read, was both enlightening and an
admonition about the fragility of freedom:

> Look to history and, when your heart saddens
> at the fact that liberty never *yet* was lasting in
> any corner of the world, and in any age, you
> will find the key of it in the gloomy truth, that
> all who yet were free regarded liberty as their
> privilege instead of regarding it as a principle.
> The nature of every privilege is exclusiveness;
> that of a principle is communicative. Liberty

is a principle—its community is its security;

exclusiveness is its doom.

Such truth in his words, and true words have power to
engender good.

I so regretted not having traveled to Boston for
Mr. Kossuth's last speech. Thus, I had to *read* his words,
rather than hear them in person as they were spoken. I
chastised myself for my inability to ignite my will with
the fuel of my fiery thoughts. My inability to do so, and
not only on this occasion, was a flaw I feel most acutely
now—I was not always able to engage my will to break
through the confines of my thoughts.

I recognized my tendency when expressed in Mr.
Shakespeare's play, *Hamlet*. The prince lamented that
thinking too much prevents action, "A thought which,
quartered, hath but one part wisdom/And ever three parts
coward." Some things we learn too late!

I was likewise moved by an image of John
Mitchel in the *Prisoners Friend*. For his efforts to obtain
justice for the Irish people; he was found "guilty" of
seditious writing as editor of the *United Irishman* and
punished with banishment by the British government
to the Bermudas for fourteen years.

As I contemplated those noble lineaments, my

*heart was filled with grief and indignation at the
tyranny of that government that has dared to pass
such a sentence in the nineteenth century. And for
what? For telling the truth and speaking out boldly
the causes of his country's wrongs, he is torn from
his family and society and sent away among outcasts
of the worse description....Ever will Erin sadly twine
for him the laurels of affection, and remember him
with the gifted and departed O'Connell.*

From this lofty perspective, I see so much
and understand even more. I myself did not work
toward such noble objectives as freedom and justice,
as Mr. Kossuth and Mr. Mitchel had, neither did I
leave great literary works of beauty and truth, as Mr.
Keats and Mr. Shakespeare had. I often did not assert
myself as I might have done, instead living more in my
thoughts and feelings.

Still, I was given a path to travel, seemingly
led by a hidden force, often without courage or
confidence and never with certainty. Mine were more
modest tasks to be carried out in my own manner and
time, albeit without the wide scope or broad impact those
and other brave and creative souls had.

And very few were my audience.

V

HOME & HEARTH

This morning I went down by the seashore.
When I came home, they had dinner all ready.
It was stewed beans and rye and Indian bread.

One might have described me as a dutiful daughter and help mate to my husband—the ideal attributes of womanhood. I was taught and practiced the skills women of my time were expected to learn and to master. Most of the daily and practical things needing attention I attended to, but did not regard them an art. They were necessities —the means to an end—washing clothes, cooking and keeping things tidy. I took more interest in tasks with tangible and beautiful results. Therefore, some skills I practiced with more enthusiasm than others.

I took great pleasure in and was quite adept at needlework, sewing a dress for a wedding, quilting a coverlet for a bed, embroidering a cloth for the table or stitching a needlepoint design to be framed. Gardening was never a chore. Sowing seeds for vegetables and herbs, tending them through the warm months, then gathering in the harvest at season's end seemed a prayer in motion.

Working in our plot overlooking Sandy Bay was most satisfying, for our hopes in the future lay there. I never tired of working in the gardens— choosing complimentary plantings of harmonious colors that would bloom together in spring, summer and then fall.

I favored the humble lily of the valley for the simple delicacy of its appearance—low growing with tiny white bells along its stems—almost hidden among wide green leaves, short lived but awaited for each May. In spring, Solomon would bring me a nosegay of them, which I would put in a little milk glass vase and place on our bedside table to lull us to sleep with their fragrance.

I was taught, learned and practiced many skills, but mastered only a few. Playing the piano was not one I had mastered to my satisfaction. Though I played often, I was not

capable of producing such sweet strains as Orpheus, who charmed the three-headed dog Cerberus by the melody of his harp, and entered the infernal regions in pursuit of his beloved Eurydice.

Yet, I continued to play for pleasure, not expecting to charm guests (or lull creatures in the underworld), but, alas, only to hear the instrument's sweet sound, *"though touched by unskilled fingers."*

Cooking was not a favorite task. Most fortunate was I then in those early years of married life that I did not have full responsibility in the kitchen. I sometimes shared in the planning and preparation of meals with Grandmother. Often, Solomon and I joined my parents next door at dinner time.

I may have been lethargic about domestic chores, but never neglected them. I did whatever was required and more, as Grandmother did so very much for our family in every way. She patiently taught me many skills, as well as passed on to me her great wisdom of life and love.

I see her still…*her peculiar dress and appearance, with a torn apron and a bonnet, a remnant of a former generation; and her queer shawl fasted by the straight edges and hanging square ways over her capacious shoulders; and her implements for gardening. She went forth—not to plant flowers, but good, substantial vegetables, such as corn, potatoes,* [and] *squash.*

There were many occasions when I unexpectedly had opportunities to learn domestic skills, as well as a thing or two about myself.

In our first years of marriage, admittedly, I may have been too dependent on Solomon, and perhaps a bit selfish. I had much to learn, and not only about home and hearth.

I am envisioning one dark, cold December evening in particular—transformed through love and cooperation, experienced now as light filled and with great warmth.

At seven o'clock I had just got things in their proper places and thrown myself into a chair. The fire was entirely out. It was quite cold. I had not courage to make one. Presently, Solomon came in. I told him I was tired, cold and hungry.

"Well, what shall I do for you?"

"I need a fire first, if anything. It is so cold and what shall we have for supper?"

"Anything, dear," I will go and make some spider cake and coffee. You may sit still and not touch a thing."

"No, no, you fix me a fire and fix me a trencher, and I will make a cake."

(There are two things Solo thinks he can do better than me. Those are to make chocolate and spider cakes— the reason he proposed them). We took down the stove when they commenced fixing the house, and I have borrowed grandmother's baker until tonight. She had company, and I didn't wish to go for it. Solomon soon came with the baker and built a great fire. I brushed the hearth and set up the cake, set the table with a clean cloth, and drew it near the fire. After everything was in readiness, I looked about me and wondered it had taken so little time to make things look this cheerful which had before seemed such a task. Solomon also remarked it. Our cake was soon done and we both sat down to our homely meal with a good relish and afterwards spent a pleasant evening.

Those were the happiest of times, spontaneous and comforting for both body and soul.

On occasion, I enjoyed the company of others, though not as much as Solomon seemed to. I preferred gatherings with my own family, which happened often and mostly at a moment's notice or by chance. It was our good fortune to be welcomed at Uncle William's guest house in Pigeon Cove. At times we were given special invitation, but also could drop in on a whim of a summer's evening to sing, play games and to engage in most interesting and varied conversation with the guests.

The times which offered most pleasure were those spent alone together. It was hard to plan time, with Solomon's work varying from day to day. Often he sailed or took the train to Boston, which brought him back later into the evening. He rarely arrived home unexpectedly or early, but when he did, we made good use of the occasion, taking a walk or a carriage ride, or working in the gardens. We also took pleasure in trying our luck at fishing any time of the day, though mostly toward evening. I preferred Norwoods Head rather than the "*grimy wharves.*"

After dinner we repaired to the sea shore with hooks and lines to catch fish. The weather was fine, and the hours flew swiftly by as we stayed by the water's edge drawing forth its finny inhabitants or watching the many sails as they passed in various directions and listening to the sounding oar.

The golden hours on angel wings,
Flew o'er me and my dearie.

Solomon delighted in pleasing me in simple ways, which endeared him to me all the more. Such it was one day in early spring when he arrived home mid-day and surprised me. I heard him calling from outside, *"Susa, come right now."* When I came to the door he said, *"Close your eyes,"* and led me outdoors. Then he whispered in my ear, *"Now, open your eyes and look."* Before me were flowering bushes, saplings of pear, plum, cherry and apple, grapevines, and English gooseberry—all of which we planted that very day at the "farm," a playful name we sometimes used for our land by the bay.

As the months passed, it brought such pride to see them flourishing and thriving in the sea air. The memory of our walking home together up the hill at dusk after a day's work, tired but contented, often sustained me when Solomon was far from me.

I look back on another special day too—one on which I was persuaded to go with him to the city.

By the earnest solicitation of my husband, I was prevailed upon to spend the day with him in Boston, in visiting the many works of art, among which was Powers' Greek Slave. Upon entering the exhibition room....My mind was humbled and subdued in the contemplation, and my soul was filled with the aspirations of genius in gazing upon that embodiment of purity and beauty which one must see to appreciate, and that words but feebly portray.

True, I had been hesitant to shift from more practical plans for the day to the unanticipated outing, which, nevertheless, was all inspiration and delight. Many were the times thereafter when simply recalling that day was as pleasant to me as the day itself— another lesson well learned.

As I have admitted, I put more thought and effort into some tasks than others; self improvement for its own sake was not one of them. Although women were expected to be dutiful daughters and wives, I was not in the habit of comparing myself with other young women. It seemed to me that some were unduly humble in that regard. In part, religious life (to which I never felt strongly drawn) encouraged worthiness in thought and deed, and partly through education, both formal and informal, women were to learn how they should live.

I was grateful for my formal education, which may have been somewhat limited for women within the mores of my time and place. I put more faith in my informally acquired education—the store of knowledge and experiences of the Norwood family and the local history and legends passed down the generations—the stories of people, places and events—some true, some not true in fact, but true in meaning.

All in all, I did come to value self-improvement, but not only because of comparisons with other women, religious teachings, family or society. Self-improvement also came through my interests—pursued and developed —and through a hard-won self knowledge, which was never achieved once and for all. It was ongoing as life unfolded year after year.

How *can* one ever quite sort through all of life's experiences, desires, motivations and fears? How *can* one fulfill all of the various expectations placed upon one from all directions? How *can* one focus on self improvement alone, with the endless daily distractions and obligations? These questions came to me when I pondered life's mysteries. I see now that if enlightenment comes at all, it comes in small doses—not at once and forever. Progress must not be measured in a straight line, and practice does not always make perfect.

I came to know more about myself and make some small movement forward (or sideways) through reflection on my experiences, especially in the things that did not go as well as expected or hoped for. Also, I became aware of qualities I admired in others—their ability to listen, to be kind, patient and compassionate.

I had to ask myself from time to time, "Can I claim to be the embodiment of those qualities in the roles I had willingly accepted as daughter, sister, wife, friend, and citizen?" Often my answer was, "No, I cannot." So, then there was the point from which to begin.

I had a great desire for knowledge throughout my lifetime and sought it through many means. I never lost enthusiasm for life or failed to learn from listening to others, reading and, of course, observing nature. I also learned to observe *myself* more closely. In certain situations I found a need to later reflect on what had occurred when more undesirable parts of myself showed themselves (and perhaps were also sensed by others). Then I have to consider a shift of some kind toward what I hoped to become and exemplify.

As I have said, I did not always welcome change and avoided participation in unexpected events or happenings, as they could be challenging to my patience and to other wished-for virtues. I had received and entertained guests many times, but depending on the company and the circumstances, receiving guests might be more of a tedious chore than a welcomed occasion.

I am remembering one year in late summer. The Packard family, not especially close friends, were coming to visit, but little did I know it would be an extended stay that would sorely try whatever patience I could manage at the time.

I knew it was impossible to procure help on such short notice and did not know what I would do to withstand the onslaught! Their visit was a triple burden: in preparation for it, during their long stay, and then later when I reflected upon how I was unable to bring to fruition my intention to develop the virtues I so admired in others.

My company have retired for the night leaving me in the enjoyment of a few moments of delicious solitude. The heat has been oppressive, and the toils of the day weighted upon me heavily. I know not what the woman can be thinking of to come among strangers with a sick child, and, if I am ever relieved of this burden, I shall think myself supremely blest.

***

Mrs.Packard's child had not been well today, and in addition to my household's affairs, I have had much to do for him so that my time has been entirely occupied with kitchen affairs—an interesting position indeed.

***

I am left alone with my insipid company...I never saw a person with so little animation. She can do nothing

or express nothing but the wants of herself and child.
I believe she is about half silly.

***

Glory, my company went this noon, and I am
once more enjoying sweet freedom.

It was so on that occasion—I simply had to do
what was required and expected with at least the
appearance of hospitality, if not its attending virtues.
Reviewing that visit was the commencement of an
awakening of sorts for me.

Although it was many years before I took up
the practice of reviewing each day before I slept, it
began with the clear realization of how I could have
managed the Packards' stay with more grace. After
that visit, sometimes before bed I would try to recall the
entire day just lived, retracing all that had happened, but
in reverse, back to my awakening in the morning.

At first, on many an evening I would fall
asleep before I got very far along. Gradually, I was
able to go further each time. This practice seemed to
elevate each new day with an awareness of my
deportment and to renew my intentions. It became
especially enlightening to recall what was most
challenging, as well as what was most welcome.

Then, I might feel grateful for a kind word or gesture from another, sometimes a stranger. Other times, it resulted in regret if I had not been able to embody those admired and desired qualities, as was the case with the Packards' visit that summer.

I discovered this practice worked better when I imagined observing myself and my circumstances from a distance, as though looking down on my world from the heights, rather like the task souls are given here.

I once heard it said, "What we practice on earth, we perfect in heaven." It is true, and in my next life I may be more able to become what I practiced in Rockport, Massachusetts.

Certainly my most common practice was seeking solitude. I do believe I perfected that on earth, as I could not go long without a quiet hour to renew my spirits. Solitude was essential, and I protected it most fiercely. Rambling in groves and on pebbled sands—those hours were mine alone and joyful. It gave me the space to see how things stood, or could be, including within myself, thereby allowing me to remember my intentions and fulfill my domestic responsibilities with a lighter heart.

At times though in my garret on a rainy afternoon, or on a long, dark evening, I would feel less at ease. The cares and woes of life, and those of others near and far edged in, transforming solitude into loneliness.

More enjoyable were those times, and they were frequent, when I cast my mind back to the rosy-colored recollections of childhood and the carefree innocence of those numbered years of youth.

But it is not alone with childhood that memory loves to linger. There are other more thoughtful hours of later years, now that I have learned to love these things, not only for their beauty, but their associations and teachings.

VI

MEMORIES & MEMENTOES

In an old manuscript, the remains of 1840 filled with mathematics, poetry, proverbs, ships under full sail, eagles on the wing, cupids, scrolls.

Although we may well know that change is inevitable, in our mind's eye, people and places remain as we once knew and remember them. However sad it may be, change comes to a once vibrant person, to a fair and youthful friend or to a beloved place we had often visited. At the mercy of age, illness, the woes of life, and the passing of time, we find an old friend unrecognizable or in despair. With changes in fortune, we may find a once stately house fallen to ruin, or a storefront in the place of a sunny garden spot we looked forward to seeing upon our return.

Time alters all things—except our longing for that which is forever lost to us.

One rainy summer night, as I waited for Solomon's arrival, I went through a small chest of treasures kept from youthful friendships—a book, a note, a trinket, a bead, a seashell, a coin. These tokens had not changed in appearance, neither had my associations with them. As I looked upon those rare remembrances and held them in my hands, I felt at once both gratitude and bittersweet nostalgia. How would the givers of those gifts appear to me? No doubt remarkably transformed, as I myself might appear to them, and not in physical form alone, but also through shifts in inner landscapes—some through small, slow movements, others through the sudden earthquakes of chance.

This evening I have been looking over friendship tokens, and as I gazed upon them each [in] succession each had its little story of love, friendship, and some of sorrow that called for tears. The associations naturally suggested the changes time had wrought upon the givers of these tiny gifts, then youths and maidens, some now men and anxious mothers.... while some I have lost sight of, but their youthful faces are deeply impressed upon my memory. Perchance we may meet again, but the ravages of time may be so great that we would pass each other by unheeded, though each lives in the other's remembrance unchanged.

There are other times, as good fortune would have it, when all might appear as first impressed upon our hearts. Such it was when Aria and I visited a friend in Folly Cove. We went through the woods and fields where, as children, we had spent many an afternoon at leisure and play. We were pleased to find our once familiar haunts just as they had lived in our memories since.

This afternoon Aria and I took the horse and buggy and went over to the Folly to see Mrs. Lane and go in the woods....It seemed almost like getting home to be amid these scenes....Each thing was welcomed as old friend, and I found them just as I love to find my friends as I left them in a year since, dressed in the same robes and beneath autumnal sunshine. Wherever I looked, it called up many sweet recollections of the past, for I have spent some of the happiest hours of my life there. We rambled around over Butlers Hill and through the woods and collected some most beautiful moss....As we came along back in the winding path through the spruce grove, I noticed our resting place, a flat rock on the verge of the thicket where we had often reclined in weariness. We sat down upon it to rest awhile in remembrance of auld lang syne, and to speak of the changes that hath come over us during the past year.

Then too, we might be amazed at unexpected but most welcome changes awaiting us in places which, hitherto, were unremarkable in every way. At the end of a summer's day, Mother, Ora and I were returning from an evening walk. Our neighbor, Mr. Parsons, invited us into his garden, once a wild pasture occupied only by boulders, rocky soil, wild brush and vines. But, O, as we entered that place of hardscrabble transformation, we were delighted to find otherwise.

The tall trees looked invitingly over the high fence, and as we entered the garden gate, the branches of the plum, heavy with fruit, bent gracefully over our heads. It was a beautiful prospect before us. The trees were thickly set in rows and heavy laden with fruit of various colors and kinds....We walked to and fro through its many paths continually coming upon something to excite our admiration....Some little trees not so high as my head bent beneath their burden of fruit. Every spot seemed turned to good account. Upon the outskirts of the garden was a large rock over which was built an arbor and upon this was a trained grape vine.

We marveled at the arbor, the thoughtfully placed rocks here and there, and the narrow, winding paths of shade and sunlight. Mr. Parsons, one of *"nature's noblemen,"* was pleased to walk us through his creation, we being complimentary all the while. Through his vision of what could be and much hard work (for it took him several years to complete), he had tamed and shaped stubborn terrain into a *"little Eden."*

So it is—there are cherished memories called to mind time and again. There are mementoes to hold in our hands and press to our hearts, bringing pleasure or pain depending on our associations with them.

I had woven a grass basket a short time before our William was born. After he was taken from us, I put it on a dark shelf in our room. In it I placed his little toy cup, the white smocked suit I made for his first birthday, and the blue booties Mother knitted for him when he was born. I managed most days not to dwell upon the loss of William. Then there were those days when I did nothing but—times when sad memories came unbidden. An intrusive thought or word could bring back the full weight of grief unaltered by time or circumstance.

On those days when I could not stem the tide, I withdrew from all company and daily tasks to my garret, took down the basket from its sheltered spot and set it on my desk by the window, next to the daguerreotype of William. Before me was the sum total of my tangible memories, and I wept over them—but more so over those not seen, but seared into my heart.

When other families also had to bear the loss of a child, it reawakened my own loss with much sympathy for and empathy with their own.

Had a letter from Uncle Richardson. Their poor little baby is dead. They are going to bring it down tonight.

***

It was buried from Grandfather's today. As I bent over the coffin and wept as I gazed upon it, it called up vividly the remembrance of that dread parting with my own darling child. I could scarce control my grief as I entered the burying ground and passed in the procession by the spot where my baby lies sleeping. I wished to break away, kneel upon the spot and pour forth my grief....Never can his place be filled in my heart. Often in the midst of joy, this thought comes up and dampens my feelings and causes the heart to start.

No matter how many years had passed, I never could speak of William's death out loud, and did not, except with Solo. Mostly, our communication was in silence—a brief glance, a touch of a hand upon the other's.

There were no words.

Then life brought me another challenge, forcing me to enlarge the scope of my grief. I would have to bear the absence of Solomon, not knowing for how long, when, or even if I would ever see him again.

It was becoming more clear that our situation was dire, as those shimmering dreams of independence in our own home were fading.

For the two past days it has stormed violently, and I have been alone and at home in the garret...busily at work on a mat. Solomon is still in Boston to collect money. I am anxious for his return fearing for his success as he stays so long. Sometimes I am near discouraged at the cloud of misfortunes seen daily thickening around us.

***

The storm hath passed away with my gloomy thoughts. I had been sitting in my garret at work on my mat until about noon, when I heard heavy footsteps approaching on the stairs. In a moment, Solomon made his appearance. I was surprised and so glad to see him, for he scarce comes home at noon....I had anxious inquiries to make about his business. He told me he had collected but little money. I asked him what he was going to do. He said nothing, but led me into the bedroom, lifted up the feather bed and drew forth long bundles containing gold in ten dollar pieces, then a pocketbook with several hundred in bills—in all amounting to twelve hundred dollars. Again and again I asked him if it was our own, fearing to believe....and he, as many times, told me they were and asked me if I did not remember his putting them there several months ago, at the time telling

*me it was mine to build our little cottage with. I
remember perfectly, but never thought of its remaining
there undisturbed when he was so pressed for money.
But now I see it drawn forth without reluctance and
give it up with a light heart to be appropriated to other
uses.*

I had once thought nothing could separate us,
but with our situation, and no prospects otherwise,
when an opportunity presented itself for Solomon to
make his mark, he was swayed to seize it. Never
would I have believed that he too, like so many others,
could be caught up in the frenzy sweeping over
Massachusetts and the whole of our country.

*Day by day, increasing interest is felt in the
news from California, our newly acquired territory
in Mexico. The cry is gold, gold; it has got to be quite
an epidemic—men both young and old are falling
victims ....The afflicted think that nothing but a visit to
the gold mine of California will reach the cause and
effectually cure.*

Then, Father Torrey offered to finance a
journey to California that would take Solomon away
for many months, maybe years. His unhappiness with
the stone business; his subsequent ventures into other
equally unsatisfactory prospects; worrisome obligations

to debtors; and his desire for our independence all persuaded him to turn elsewhere to seek his fortune.

When I first apprehended his intention, a cloud of gloom hovered over me, as one year was ending and a new one was about to begin—one promising only sadness and uncertainty.

I gave Solomon my admonition against his even *thinking* of going away and tried to push my own thoughts on it to the back of my mind, as I had tried to do with the loss of William. I was resolved to look toward preparations for the Christmas holiday—a joyous time for celebration and fellowship. Such activity, I had hoped, would occupy me and distract me from the darkness descending.

Mother is preparing for Christmas. We took supper and spent the evening with them. Cummins talks of going to California. As for Solomon, I have forbidden his speaking or even thinking of the thing.

***

It's Christmas the last yearly festival. Today many friends will meet to join in social mirth. Families that have been separated for months will be called together beneath the parental roof to taste home joys. So is it at my home....Father and Mother have made bountiful preparations for the meeting together of their children. I am about to join them.

A splendid day and week it has been—quiet evenings with Solomon, warm gatherings at Mother's—holly and greens on the table and at the windows, candles on the tree, and our exchange of happy wishes and small gifts—lovely!

A dance was held at the ballroom on December 26, but a shadow was cast over the evening. My sister, Aria, was disappointed to find that her Cummins would not attend the gathering. His father's "scruples" forbade dancing! Solomon, ever the gentlemen insisted, nevertheless, that Aria come with us and promised to dance with her. She declined and stayed home, dejected.

Later we found out that Cummins had entertained himself that very evening with friends, smoking cigars at E. Tufts' store! Still, their friendship persisted though marked with various episodes of concern from the Haskell and the Norwood families, myself included.

Despite my vow not to think any further of Solomon's leaving and busying myself with the holiday festivities, a low but clear dirge sounded which I could not ignore. At day's end before sleep, worries stubbornly edged their way into my thoughts during what should have been restful hours. The approach of each new year, in any case, had always been wont to put me into a melancholy state—with disbelief at how quickly a year passes.

And so I existed for that time between the season's good cheer, with wishes for peace and good will toward men, and the dread of what might lie ahead in the new year.

VII

EBB & FLOW

*Hope sometimes gleams brightly in a distance and pictures a
better future and tells me all will be well. But these bright
gleams are transient.*

*A new era has commenced—the old year has passed
away, but its memory still remains fraught with
a thousand memorable recollections. Misfortune's hand
had been laid heavily upon us. Still, we have seen much
happiness. Solomon and myself have been together
more than upon any previous year since our marriage.
Since giving up the stone business, his work has been
very near home....Fortune has gone. After giving up the
business, Solomon did not know the extent of our losses
....The extent of our misfortune has come upon us
gradually....We have health and scorn not to labor, but
Solomon was never made to fill any common sphere.
His mind would never be satisfied with plodding on
from day to day to accumulate wealth for the sake of
living in indolence or to hoard away with miser's care,
but as a means of cultivating his taste for the sublime
and beautiful that ever reigned predominant in his soul.
And he is not alone in his aspirations. But I fear the day
is far distant when these fond hopes will be realized. The
prospect before me looks gloomy.*

At first the new year brought occasional mentions of a journey to California, then plans—formulated and discussed, in which I did not participate. The gloomy cloud I had sensed above me was descending with a darkness I could not see past. My heart was almost broken when, before a family supper one evening in late January, Mother said to me,

"Solomon says he is going to California, Susa."

"He loves to talk about it, but he does not think of it, and I will not let him go unless he takes me."

Solomon chimed in,*"That would be impossible Susa....What can I do here? I will go by the Isthmus. You can hear from me often, and I will come home in the fall if you say so."*

"O, Solomon, I beg, you will not say anything more about it, for I cannot consent to let you go," and I almost burst into tears. Presently he arose saying he was going down to see to the horse and would soon return.

It came to me with full force then. I was the *only* one opposed to what by then seemed a completed plan. Solomon left the room, no doubt to allow Mother to talk some sense into me, or so they had hoped, also so he would not have to see the sorrow engendered in me by the thought of our separation. When Solomon was gone, Mother put her arm around my shoulder and tried to reason with me. She reminded me that husbands have ever left their wives to improve their lot, and a year would pass quickly. Though other years had always seemed to fly into the next, I knew a year without Solomon would not seem so. I was not comforted in the least, and I did not understand such reasoning; "*silent tears*" were my response.

Despite awareness of my disapproval and sadness, within a few days, Solomon told me he had accepted his father's offer to fund a voyage. With Father Torrey's blessing and the means to go, a vessel was being prepared to sail around Cape Horn into the Pacific, then north to California with Solomon and a company of nine other men from Cape Ann aboard.

The journey to their destination could take months and, I knew, would be threatened by many dangers besides encounters with rough seas, certain at some point along the way. There could also be illness, shortage of food, supplies and all manner of entirely unforeseen hazards, including long delays in ports, which would further prolong Solo's absence.

These and other fears crowded my mind day and night until I felt paralyzed, knowing the trip was a fait accompli, with or without my consent. Although Solomon's and my family were concerned for my well being, they also looked for the smallest sign of my making peace with the voyage. Though from the beginning I had not wavered, neither sanctioning nor colluding in the conspiracy, a time came when I could protest no longer. I did not wish to be obstinate while around me all necessary preparations commenced. To continue remaining opposed to my husband's wishes and intentions then seemed foolish. The grand plan would soon be carried out.

Even though the date for sailing had been set, when Father Torrey visited, he took me aside and kindly asked, *"Well, Susannah, are you going to let Solomon go to California?"*

"I don't know," was all I could reply, knowing there was nothing to be done. I turned away and went into the next room to hide my sorrow. Later, I came back to spend time with Father Torrey during his afternoon visit, but neither he nor I spoke of my "letting" Solomon go, or my sadness.

When Solomon came home the following day, he asked me to sit with him. I wanted to say, "No, no, I will not; just go now if you must leave, " and at the same moment I wanted to cling to him. What did anything matter? The thought of our parting was more than I could bear. How could there be *anything* without him?

Still, I agreed to sit with him, after which I felt a turning within myself from desperately wanting everything to remain as it had been—toward the clear and present reality that *everything* was about to change.

Solomon came in and sat down in the great rocking chair and asked me to come and sit with him. He took me in his arms and kissed me affectionately ...as he told me the necessity of the present step. He said were he situated as we were a year ago, he would not think of it, but without suitable business, but little money and few friends, he knew nothing better.... The only thing unpleasant was the thoughts of parting with me, and he then pressed me still closer to his bosom and told of his affection for me. How sincerely my heart responded! He has ever been generous and kind to me nor never denied me of anything since we have been married. Not never did either of us close our eyes in sleep with a hard thought of the other. Can I part with such a treasure? My heart tells me no, for I almost worship him.

I can proudly say that amid all his enemies have said against him, none have dared speak ill of his moral character. He will go forth with my entire confidence. It is the thought of absence, dangers and hardships that weigh so heavily.

The following weeks passed quickly. The days grew short with the darkness of mid-winter. The nights were long with cold winds and a few snow storms. I had ceased writing in my diary, as I busied myself tidying the house, baking mince pies with Mother, and slowly gathering what was needed for my husband's long journey—those dreaded tasks.

The time draws near. Most everything is in readiness....[I am] *feeling like one laboring under some deep and unavoidable calamity.*

Solomon occupied himself with preparations of his own, accepting whatever work he was offered to help fund the journey, some of which were treacherous—helping to remove a wreck ashore on Ten Pound Island. He received twenty-five dollars for the work there, and eighteen dollars from Mother Torrey, who had been saving on her own.

All too soon the time was upon us to say farewell. When I again began to write in my diary, I wondered if anyone at some future time would read the thoughts recorded, and sense the depth and weight of sorrow expressed therein.

We were very busy all of the evening in packing his clothes. The family were in and out until ten o'clock when we were left alone to spend an hour in the interchange of kind words and pledges of affection, recalling the past with it joys and sorrows....I gave him a little tin dipper that was our darling baby's. He received it gratefully, for it was one of his last playthings.

He asked me for the uncased daguerrotype of our darling. As we gazed upon the sweet face of our little boy and wept for the treasure we once with joy could call our own, the loss came back to me with double force. I could have better borne this last deep sorrow were our baby here to soothe and comfort. In the morning, I awoke with a groan....Were I doomed to die, I should not have felt a deeper misery.

The morning of Solomon's departure dawned. We awoke very early, but remained in our chamber until Grandmother called us for breakfast. As we sat together, I thought of the many happy times we had spent with family and friends at the table. Then, I could not help but think that this may be our last meal together. As Solomon tried to distract me, unabashedly

I hung over him crying aloud. He asked me to put up a piece of cake that he might have when he was far away. He said it would taste so sweet...because his little Susa made it.

Then we went to gather the last of his cases, and alone for the brief time left to us, we held each other until we heard Grandfather call to say all was ready. We left our room aware that the sacred moments just shared would have to tide us over long months and span thousands of miles. Hand in hand, we went to join the others waiting below.

He pressed me to his bosom, kissed me for the last time, and with a sudden effort started from me. He went but a few steps and hesitated, cast one sad look behind. I know his thoughts. He would return. It was but a moment and he was gone from my sight.

Presently, I heard Grandfather say, "God bless you," and the carriage roll over the stone pavements.

Unavoidable change was then upon me. Even as life went on in much the same way with responsibilities and daily tasks, I didn't know how *I* would go on? My focus on everything was blurred. The rhythm and purpose of life seemed distorted with all of its parts awry, scattered, or missing. I had the strange sense of time slowing down as I attempted to live my old, new life in sadness.

Would anything ever be as it once was? I thought not—knowing, how with even a small change, nothing ever quite returns to what it had been. My family thought it better that I move from my grandparents' to my parents' house next door, where I would again share a room with Aria, as I had before I married. Although I hesitated at first, I then agreed. Yes, it surely would be better to move from the place Solomon and I had shared as man and wife—now apart. To go back was hard to bear, but I looked forward with whatever determination I could muster to accept yet another change.

Swept my chamber and arranged the furniture so that it looks quite pretty. I have more than two-thirds of my things moved, and, for the life of me, I do not see where I am going to stow them.

The forward movement of life as mother had ceased long before and then as wife had come to an abrupt halt, though not to an end was my fervent hope. Indeed, I felt the sharp sting of it all, even as I was truly grateful to have my family near. I resolved to devote the part of me that had been wife to be of help to them.

Solomon and I had vowed to write to each other often. I looked forward to hearing the news, as the days passed, but still no letter had arrived.

Evening. I am very sad and anxious to hear from Solomon, for I have seen many accounts of storms and shipwrecks on the course they have taken. They have been gone five weeks—it seems time that I should hear from him. O, that I would know where [he] is at this moment, or that I could be with him even to suffer death if shared with him, for life is nothing without him. The hope that we shall meet again is all that cheers my

sinking spirit and arouses me to action. If this be dashed
from me, ambition and every other hope will die, and
every wish to live will cease.

When Solomon's letters finally began to arrive,
they recounted his many new and varied experiences.
Depending on the news, my worries and fears diminished
or grew greater. The first letters came from New York,
then from ports along the way. All in the same long letter
there would be conflicting expressions of humor and
sadness, certainty and doubt, but always a note of hope
for the future, which kept me from despair, for "hope is a
thing with feathers."

He often conveyed tender thoughts, expressing
his longing for me. He sometimes wrote of his memories
of home with new realizations of deep appreciation for
our parents' generosity, concern and loving support of
our union, and the many sacrifices they had made for us.

I had a letter with mention of a recent illness, of
the discomforts of the voyage, and of disturbing things
he saw while held over in Panama—others living and
working in situations very different from what we knew
in our lives on Cape Ann. Solomon wrote:

I never knew what misery was until I came out to
the Isthmus. The government keeps their prisoners to

work lugging stone and wood on their backs and makes
them wear a large chain....Shackled together, then they
are followed around by a soldier with a loaded gun...
When they punish their children they beat them terribly,
their naked bodies and knock them over and kick them
around.

I read his words but wished I had not learned of such things, though true and real. The scene came to life before me and imprinted itself upon my soul, as if I myself had witnessed it. I began to see that what Solomon had to learn and bear along the way would be part of his growth and independence, just as enduring the life I had to live without him would be for me.

Would we, could we, ever be the same with and for each other?

We each wrote long letters in which we seemed compelled to relate all we saw, thought, felt and did in the time between our last letter and the present one, as if to create in words what did not exist in reality. Often his news was tempered with reassuring notes, such as when he wrote of ships coming out of California with tales of gold, which boosted his spirits for a time.

There was a brig just arrived from California
....I saw the Captain. He tells a large story about the

gold. He had some specimens which he exhibited, one piece in particular that would weigh about two pounds.

***

More good news. The steamer Oregon *has just arrived from California. She brings good news from the gold regions together with a plenty of gold. The passengers say there is no mistake but there is a plenty of gold, but it is bad getting up where it is. There is one gentlemen here that has a piece of gold that he says will weigh 8 pounds. A number of passengers say they have enough to last them a lifetime. They appear to be pretty happy.*

I hoped they were not tall tales and that there had been, after all, not only good reason for Solomon to have gone away, but also that he would return, if not with gold to last a lifetime, then at least enough for the risk he had taken so our separation would not have been in vain.

Once settled in my childhood home, living again with my parents and sister, I would be awake when Aria came in to tell me of evenings with her Cummins. Her smiles and overflowing happiness reminded me of my own carefree time when Solomon and I had entertained

dreams of a brilliant future. I would rather add than take from her cup of bliss, but visions of the past

*came back to me....each fond hope is blighted. I am
again in the home of my childhood, but not with the
same light heart that I left it: I am sad and lonely now.
Youth and fortune has fled. Our baby is laid in the silent
grave, and my husband is in a distant land.*

Amid such experiences and thoughts, I became
aware of additional responsibilities—some of which I
felt I must take on; others I freely chose. I had the
feeling of expanding into something new and different—
I supposed it was a growing independence—neither
asked for, nor much welcomed. I also perceived the
smallest, but dark place in me—one of resentment for
Solomon's having chosen a prolonged separation. I
feared there would be a knot in the fabric of our
marriage.

Everything was different, alas, changed, as I had
always been wont to avoid, though I never stopped
missing him or wondering if, indeed, I would see him
again. His letters remained alternately worrisome and
encouraging. I struggled to cope with the many new and
shifting feelings of my new situation.

I had heard absence from or worry about loved
ones may cause a person to imagine things out of a
strong desire to have them near. I remembered hearing
about an old woman who had lived in our town, and

who had lost her son in the Revolutionary War. To the end of her days, the story went, she would see him walk past her window at dusk dressed in his uniform, as if arriving home again. She would hear a knock at the door, but when she answered it, no one was there.

Something happened to me that I do *not* believe was my imagination, so intense and vivid was the experience. I was planting seeds for a flower garden on a lovely day in spring, and thinking of Solomon, but not with a heavy heart. My mind was clear, like the skies. The ground whereon I knelt was warm, and a crisp breeze blew off Sandy Bay.

I heard a rustling behind me like someone approaching. My first thought was that it was Solomon, turning, I saw his face. It wore a pleasant roguish expression, just as it often had when he was trying to steal upon me unexpectedly. In turning, my hood slipped part way over one side of my forehead. I put up my hand to push it away, but the bright vision was gone I knew not how, and left me to wonder.

Had Solomon also seen me at the same moment, wherever he was? It did not seem a vision, but real, and a comfort. It remained in my mind as more than an odd, imaginary happening. I neither forgot it, nor ever doubted it.

Gardening, as always, brought me a small measure of peace, and I continued to collect mosses to arrange into designs for my scrapbooks—my prized work. It brought me much pleasure to see the delicacy and grace of an arrangement, and much serenity to recall the quiet hours spent finding them. I still made time to become part of what had always been more real to me than anything else. Beside the calm coves was a kind of tranquility—not found elsewhere.

A most peaceful feeling also would come over me late in the quiet of evening just before sleep with only the sound of the sea. One night I was awakened and surprised by an unusual happening right outside my window.

I had just fallen asleep, when I was awakened by a sweet strain of music. My first impression was that it was some beautiful dream, but gathering my scattered senses, I soon began to think it a reality. I arose, lifted the curtain, and sat down by the open window—just below stood the minstrels, three in number, pouring forth their rich deep voices in a sweet sentimental strain accompanied by a Spanish guitar and violin ....The words seemed strangely appropriate."To my love that's far away,"....I sat long after the last strain had died away....The moon rode high in the azure heavens, shedding its pale light over reposing nature. The air was

*still and clear, and the ocean made strange music in its
regular ebb and flow on the pebbly shore.*

Although I still sought quiet and solitude, I did
not wish to remain idle. I devoted much of my time to
sewing projects: dresses, coverlets, and quilts, some for
which I received recompense. Though I had always done
so, working to create practical but beautiful things
became more enjoyable. I looked forward to beginning a
project and, once begun, I would do nothing else but
work until it was completed—sometimes on the same
day.

At first I had taken on sewing to help pay a
portion of Solomon's debts while he was gone, but it

soon became a most welcome and rewarding endeavor, more so than a necessity. There was an increasing stream of inquiries from family, friends and even from mere acquaintances about whatever skills I possessed as a seamstress. I experienced genuine appreciation for my designs and finely finished garments.

I began to fall into a new rhythm of life, yet continued to participate in things Solomon and I would have done together—a carriage ride on a Sunday afternoon, but then with Mother or Aria; enjoyment of our town's glorious celebration of Independence Day, a favorite of Solomon's; or accepting an invitation to a social gathering. I enjoyed these activities for themselves and was happy for opportunities to amuse and distract myself. But part of my heart's joy was reserved for Solomon alone, even in the midst of a crowd.

Friends invited Aria and me to the Mount Pleasant Boarding House for a party, where we were such a mixed company composed of various classes, such as doctors, ministers, Boston merchants and dash clerks and many ladies. The gentlemen threw aside their dignity for the time and joined with real zest in the noisy games of the evening. But the ladies were more exacting, each claiming the imagined respect due to their respective class....After our games were over, we had some fine singing by some ladies from Andover.

I wrote to Solomon of all the people, places and events which had been part of our lives together. At times, when reading his letters, I felt as though we were sitting beside each other at the hearth after a long day, such was the familiarity of our exchanges. We often wrote of our fond recollections of times we had spent together.

O, Susannah,

If I could be down to your father's table this noon with you on one side of me and your Father, Mother and Aria there at the same time with a good dish of your pork and greens,...wouldn't I enjoy it? And in the afternoon have you, Ora, Aria [and] *Mother go down and catch a mess of Cunners for supper, would not that be real nice, Susa?*

Solomon and I seemed to have that ease in conversation from the first afternoon we met. In every-day practical affairs we used ordinary language, but in matters of the heart and more lofty thoughts, our words were more intimate, more lyrical, as they came from deep within us.

When I wrote of nature in my diary, it seemed as if something flowed from me which wrote itself. Solomon also had the capacity for such eloquence, but only with regard to his affection for me, which I could then "hear" only in his letters. In my desk drawer I kept a gift he gave me on the first anniversary of our marriage. I felt myself the most fortunate woman in the wide world to have received it. On our bed that morning, he left a parchment scroll with a single stem of lily of the valley from our garden—bound with a green ribbon. Therein, he had written thoughts so lovely:

> To My Darling Susa,
> If life is but a dream, and we
> dreamers on earth's green velvet mantle
> our thoughts, then, transcend this sleep
> and only we, my love,
> know the thoughts hidden there.
>
> From Your Solomon

This gift I took out to read many times during Solomon's absence, and each year on the anniversary of our union—until the end of my life.

The days, weeks and months passed. When Solomon had been with me, I did not mind the long evening hours in the quiet of the house. I would eagerly anticipate being alone. As I awaited Solomon's arrival, I spent that time in reverie, or writing in my diary. In his absence, however, the evenings often brought an unfamiliar apathy and emptiness.

The evening has been the dullest thing imaginable. The family have all retired for the night.

The clock has just struck eleven. I am alone in my chamber seated at my writing table....I have thrown aside my dress, put on a loose sack, bid farewell to combs and hairpins (that is for tonight) and have been scribbling this two hours as if for dear life. Who will pay me? No one sure. The bright stars look down lovingly, and the soft breezes are wooing me to a seat by the open window. So farewell pen, ink and paper.

I had always been welcome to visit Mother and Father Torrey in Quincy, but I seldom took up their kind invitation. I visited on one occasion for an extended stay while Solomon was away, and his sister Joanna came to Rockport to visit me more than once.

On a beautiful day in August, Joa and I spent the afternoon picking berries and roaming in Shoemaker Grove where we gathered branches of blossoms, mosses and grasses to make arrangements later.

As we left the grove and entered the adjoining wood, I turned to take a parting look. There is a pleasant reminiscence connected with those dark old rocks in the background of a long sunshiny summer's afternoon spent upon their heights overlooking the ocean, the valley and surrounding woods.

We then took a long walk around a familiar hill to a favorite vantage point I wanted to show Joa. Though we cared much for one another, Joa and I, we were far apart in the way we perceived and thought about things, which often made for lively conversation, but not on this occasion.

Very often I love to go and linger in this very spot and live over in memory the happy hours spent there. Each diverging path leads to some little altar that claims a tribute of affection. A tide of recollections come rushing o'er me filling my whole heart with pleasure. I asked Joa what she thought of it. She looked around and very cooly replied she thought it a common scene. She could see no particular beauty there. I was so surprised and disappointed, for I love to hear the praises of the things that please me so.

This incident affected me with a longing for the only person whom I felt understood and truly knew me. At that moment, it seemed as if married life had never existed. Was a woman still a wife if her husband is no longer with her to share in life together?

I was growing more independent—what choice did I have? I was meeting with admiration and appreciation for my needlecraft, which was reward enough, but the money I earned from it allowed me to pay off some of our debt, as well as to buy something for myself from time to time. It was clear to me, and I had to confess to Solomon that I had found profitable and pleasant work.

Solo had "*forbidden me to work*," but when I told him of my new "occupation," he had to feign displeasure, and gently reprimanded me in one of his letters, calling me a "*little rogue and a confounded dear.*" I knew, nevertheless, he was proud of my efforts and grateful for my contribution to diminish our debt, which helped to restore his pride and his reputation, both of which had been at stake.

Perhaps he too had feared our life together would not be the same when we came together again. Neither of us wrote of such things to the other. We may not have been certain if the *same* would be possible, but we also could not guess that *different* would not be at all tragic, and would be just as pleasing.

Over the months, there were hints of change in Solomon. I sensed in the content and tone of his letters a new determination, a more mature voice—more confident to meet the many challenges in *his* new life. He was facing and withstanding hardships with growing strength and courage. He was apparently willing and able to see things through to their conclusion, even if it might mean more time away than we had hoped.

And so, our lives went on apart from the other. We had endured until, alas, Solomon did come back to me, although not with gold *"enough to last a lifetime."* Before he left California, he even had to suffer the indignity of once again cutting stone in order to help finance the return voyage—what he had been so unhappy with before he journeyed afar.

The days before Solomon's return were full, with preparations and with anticipation—part fearful, part joyful. Simply imagining our reunion seemed strange to me and filled me with many apprehensions.

On the day he arrived home, he was greeted and welcomed by our families, and neighbors who came and went all through the day, which made our initial meeting more formal and less strained. There were tears, good humor, and laughter all around. Solomon good-naturedly answered many questions and told amazing tales of men ruined and men made wealthy.

He looked different—thinner and tired, but he was my Solomon. When we were finally alone in the evening, our reunion was as if meeting for the first time. Our embrace was warm and familiar, somewhat reserved but happy, very happy.

By morning, all of the long-empty places within us were brimful.

The resentment I once felt had diminished by then, almost as if it had been felt by someone else—the someone I used to be. We were not different in our mutual affection and were able to enjoy each other's more mature and more independent self. We had to learn to appreciate each other in a new way—the way we had become living without the other.

Together we still held the promise of an unfulfilled dream. Though we had been apart for so long, with love's golden thread stretched across distance and time, it had not broken and became ever so bright again —for the short time we had left.

VIII

REFLECTION & REVERIE

If life is but a dream, and we are said to be dreamers…
our thoughts then transcend this sleep.

"Now," "here"—I must use those words so you will understand—you who live in time and space, you who have experience of a now and a then, a here and a there. I do not. I will try to open to you some of the truths and the necessities revealed to those waiting between death and rebirth.

We acutely feel what we brought into being on account of our untruths, our thoughtlessness, our unkindness, and all manner of other indiscretions and transgressions during our lifetimes. All things, no matter how small or seemingly insignificant, are of consequence and have implications, both in this realm and through our next incarnation.

Often what I experienced in life gave me intimations of what I find to be true on the other side. One such apprehension came to me while reading *Hamlet,* in the words of King Claudius, who murdered his own brother and took both crown and queen from him. When his conscience is stirred, he attempts to pray for forgiveness, but is not willing to give up what he gained from his sin. He laments that there may be impunity in *this* world,

> …but tis not so above;
> There is no shuffling, there the action lies
> In his true nature; and we ourselves compell'd,
> Even to the teeth and forehead of our faults,
> To give in evidence. What then?

Mr. Shakespeare illuminated the unalterable. The "what then" can be terrible. There *is* a reckoning—though not in a fiery pit. We experience our own transgressions exactly as others felt them, and, O, the waves of burning remorse are pain enough.

Mercifully, we also are bathed in a brilliant, warm light with revelations of how we helped others through our kindness, sacrifice and compassion; how we brought joy or comfort; how we saved someone from despair, or even death—all forgotten since by us, or unbeknownst to us at the time.

It seems I gained some measure of knowledge during my lifetime through both the joyous and the sorrowful. I often sensed the embodiment of truth, goodness and beauty in others, and in works of art, music and literature—and always in blessed nature. I grew in appreciation for the imaginative element in life—the ability to see through and beyond the ordinary, and was grateful to be part of all I experienced and to ever be inspired by it.

I once read in Greek mythology about a river of forgetfulness from which waiting souls drink before birth. It is true! With each new birth, we forget what came before. All memory fades, but between lives we see, know and remember, as we prepare to return. Yet, our previous lives' memories and deeds will direct us in our next earthly existence—though we will not remember why we have come and what we are to do.

Nevertheless, the circumstances into which we are born; our desires; our relationships with others; and all our experiences, especially those that lift and expand our consciousness, will lead us to our destinies each time

On earth I had intuited a consciousness beyond life, though I was never certain how it would be or what it would mean after death. If we are intuitive and open to all there is, we may develop a sense for what is being spoken to us from a previous life, as well as from the present one.

We must listen, then, and strive to understand the words and deeds of loved ones, and all others—near and far—friend and foe alike. We must imagine ourselves in the place of others. It matters here that we were able to withhold our judgment and condemnation, yet it was ever a struggle for me to do so, with many failures until the very end. We may often fail in our efforts, but, it is the striving toward the good, the beautiful and the true that counts.

We must also be aware of, if not always able to heed, our own hearts' desires, separating the illusions of them from the right motivations for them. Our lives form a pattern—a theme permeating our existence in various forms and situations. If we can discern it, then we may know where to look for direction. Most of all, we can learn to read the Book of Nature with its many correspondences to our humanity—hidden or in plain view. There is much to be learned from the voice of the earth and from the regal heavens above.

In my lifetime in Rockport, I intuited bits of wisdom here and there—glimpsed as rays of light in the darkness. I am recalling one in particular, expressed by poet, Sarah Edgarton Mayo, who "*has left her beautiful spirit, with which we can hold sweet communion,*" as I did on earth, and still do, with Sarah Allen, "*an intelligent and beautiful lady and dearly loved friend.*"

Mrs. Allen is no more. She removed to Boston… and, whilst there, became insane and put an end to her life. O, that I had never known her fate, for, ever when thinking of her, these sad thoughts intrude themselves upon those pleasant memories. I have a book she gave me, The Rose of Sharon, *and among the many gifts of friends, none is more highly prized than this.*

Mrs. Allen's gift to me was by no mere chance. In it was a poem by Mrs. Mayo in which I sensed a truth —one confirmed to me in this place of waiting. The wisdom therein not only eased the pain of Sarah's death at the time, but also filled me with gratitude for her life, and for my own.

> The mind is like a torch that through the gloom
> Sheds a clear brightness where our feet should tread;
> O blessed lot, from altar to the tomb,
> By hand and heart so steadfast to be led!

Epilogue

After Solomon and I were reunited, almost at once we again took up the plans to build our stone cottage. As it rose up, stone upon stone, so did the old rumor— discovery of pirate gold at Gully Point by my great grandfather, Caleb Norwood. I neither confirmed nor denied it during my lifetime, and even now will not tell whether it be truth or no.

Once only a dream, our kingdom by the sea came into being in the midst of the color and light of sea and sky surrounding it.

All of our trees and gardens were planted with so much thought and great care—some long before the granite foundation was placed. A few of the gardens spoke the language of flowers: lily of the valley for return of happiness, strawflowers for never-ceasing remembrance, and delphiniums for well being.

From every window facing the sea was a view of one special garden under the shelter of a weeping cherry tree, in memory of our beloved child, William. Beneath its branches grew graceful ferns, bright perennials and ground cover, dotted with tiny white flowers that shone like stars in the moonlight.

Alongside this tree—a granite monument on a blanket of moss, and beyond it—the watchful sea.

Once again we became a family, as we welcomed two beautiful daughters, Susannah and Aria. But only five years after he came back to me, I had to bid farewell to my Solomon again—for the last time.

We had just those brief but full and happy years.

Thereafter, I lived a long life of widowhood, all in our little town of Rockport which, along with me, saw and withstood many changes, even the onslaught of the twentieth century. Our daughters grew up in a very different world than we had known. It was great comfort to have left them with the wisdom passed on to me from Mother and Grandmother, and with the legacy of their Norwood ancestors—hardy and courageous souls, like Francis who had come so far, so long ago. He and his descendants lived decent lives of hard work and sacrifice, leaving a rich family history and their contributions to the life of Cape Ann, where our daughters also lived their lives and raised families of their own.

Until the end, I never tired of solitude. I was never lonely.

Our stone cottage still stands—a testament to love and perseverance and to the lives lived in our earthly paradise.

The lights from the beacon glimmered in a distance and our little boat was lost in the darkness when we arose and bent our steps homeward toward the village over which the shades of night were fast gathering.

ILLUSTRATIONS
by Robert Louis Williams
www.robertlouiswilliams.com

Acknowledgements & Notes

Cover

Portrait of Susannah Norwood Torrey at age 17, painted
by Alfred J. Wiggin (1823–1883), a Massachusetts artist
known for his portraiture and landscapes.

Dedication

"But if the while I think on thee,…/All losses are restored and
sorrows end." - Shakespeare from Sonnet 30.

Paradise

Page 3: "covered with trees of different sorts…." - quote
from Champlain in Saville, Marshall, H. *Champlain and His
Landings on Cape Ann 1605, 1606.*
Note: The inscription on the historical marker near Whale
Cove on South Street, Rockport, MA: "Due east from here on
July 16, 1605, the Sieur De Monts sent Samuel de Champlain
ashore to parley with some Indians. They danced for him and
traced an outline map of Massachusetts Bay. These French
explorers named this promontory The Cape of Islands."

Page 4: "Here every man may be master and owner of his
owne labour and land…." - quoted from John Smith's
guidebook to New England in Saville, Marshall, H.
Champlain and His Landings on Cape Ann 1605-1606.

Page 5: "le beau port" - Champlain sailed into Gloucester
Harbor on his second trip to Cape Ann in 1606 and referred
to it as "le beau port."

Page 6: "kingdom by the sea" - Edgar Allan Poe from "Annabel Lee."

Page 6: "the paradise of all those parts I have seen…." quoted fromJohn Smith's guidebook to New England in Saville, Marshall, H. *Champlain and His Landings on Cape Ann 1605-1606.*

SOLITUDE & SOLICITUDE

Page 28: "When old age shall this generation waste…" - John Keats from "Ode on a Grecian Urn."

Page 30: "wider than the sky" - Emily Dickinson from "The Brain is Wider than the Sky" in *Poems by Emily Dickinson, First & Second Series,* edited by Mabel Loomis Todd and T. W. Higginson.

Page 34-35: "Look to history…." - "Kossuth's Last Speech in Fanueil Hall." *Kossuth in New England: Full Account of the Hungarian Governor's Visit to Massachusetts.*
NOTE: Louis Kossuth was a Hungarian statesman invited by the Commonwealth of Massachusetts to visit and speak throughout New England and New York.

Page 35: "A thought which, quartered…" - William Shakespeare from *Hamlet* (4.4).

Page 35: *Prisoner's Friend* - a monthly publication devoted to criminal reform, philosophy, science, literature and art. Boston, MA: Charles Spear, John M. Spear,1845-1857?

HOME & HEARTH

PAGE 49: "What we practice on earth, we perfect in heaven."
unknown source

EBB & FLOW

Page 71: "hope is a thing with feathers" - Emily Dickinson
from "Hope" in *Poems by Emily Dickinson, First & Second
Series,* edited by Mabel Loomis Todd and T. W. Higginson.

REFLECTION & REVERIE

Page 87: "…but tis not so above…" - William Shakespeare
from *Hamlet* (3.3).

Page 90: "The mind is like a torch through the gloom…" -
Sarah Edgarton Mayo, excerpt from "Thou Art Formed to
Guide."
NOTE: Mayo (1819~1848) of Gloucester, MA, was a writer,
poet, and an editor of *The Rose of Sharon,* a Universalist
publication of religious and literary writings. Her complete
works were published posthumously by her husband Armor
Dwight Mayo, a clergyman.

References

Callam, G. Marion Norwood. *The Norwoods II: A Chronological History.* Bexhill-on-Sea. East Sussex, England: published by the author, 1997.

Cressy, David. *Coming Over: Migration and Communication Between England and New England in the Seventeenth Century.* Cambridge, UK: Cambridge University Press, 1987.

"Kossuth's Last Speech in Fanueil Hall," *Kossuth in New England: A Full Account of the HungarianGovernor's Visit to Massachusetts: with His Speeches and Addresses Made to Him.* Boston, Massachusetts: John P. Jewett & Co. Cleveland, Ohio: Jewett, Proctor, and Worthington,1852.

Mayo, Sarah Edgarton. "Thou Art Formed to Guide." American Female Poets [an electronic edition]. http://quod.lib.umich.edu/a/amverse/ BAE7433.0001.001/1:64?rgn=div1;view=fulltext.

Norwood, Maureen. *Francis Norwood, Immigrant to Massachusetts: and His Descendants 1635-1987.* Baltimore, Maryland: Gateway Press, 1987.

Painter, Lucy Butler, editor. *Diary of Susannah Norwood Torrey: A Feminine Reflection of Mid-Nineteenth Century Rockport.* Bethany, Connecticut: published by the editor (Blurb), 2003.

Parsons, Eleanor. *Fish, Timber, Granite & Gold*. Researched by Peter Bergholtz and Donald Dawson. Sponsored by Sandy Bay Historical Society and Museums: Rockport, Massachusetts, 2003.

Pool, Ebenezer. *Ebenezer Pool Papers: Volumes 1-VI* Original Manuscripts, Rockport,Massachusetts: Collection of Sandy Bay Historical Society, 1822-1870.

Saville, Marshall H. *Champlain and His Landings on Cape Ann 1605, 1606*. American Antiquarian Society, 1933. Collection of Sandy Bay Historical Society.

Smith, John."A Description of New England" (1616). *Zea E-Books in American Studies,* Book 3.

Swan, Marshall W. S. *Town on Sandy Bay: A History of Rockport, Massachusetts*. Canaan, New Hampshire: Phoenix Publishing, 1980.

Thanks & Gratitude

To Gwen Stephenson and Judy Bogage at Sandy Bay Historical Society and Museums, Rockport, MA, for their assistance with research.

To Lucy Butler Painter, a descendant of the Norwood family, for sharing information with me about her research for her edited publication of *Diary of Susannah Norwood Torrey: A Feminine Reflection of Mid-Nineteenth Century Rockport.*

To Shelley Brandenburger, a descendant of the Norwood family, for meeting with me and sharing her knowledge of Norwood history and her family documents.

To Betsy and Frank Eck, Innkeepers of The Inn on Cove Hill, Rockport, MA, for taking me through the rooms in which Susannah lived and wrote.

To my fellow writers and friends at the Finish Line writers' group in Gloucester, MA: Barbara Boudreau, Stacey Dexter, Dan Duffy, Cindy Hendrickson, Jane Keddy, John Mullen, and Cindy Schimanski, for their support and encouragement.

Images of notes and dried flowers are from the pages of Susannah's Album of Botanical Specimens - at Sandy Bay Historical Society and Museums, Rockport, MA

About the Author

SANDRA WILLIAMS taught Language Arts, World Literature, and Reading, Writing & Research for over twenty-five years at both high school and university levels. Having always written poetry and essays (*New View Magazine,* UK), she has now authored *Moss on Stone* and *Time and Tide: a collection of tales.*

Sandra loves living on beautiful Cape Ann, with her artist husband Robert. Both are inspired by its beauty and its community of creativity. She is a member of the Finish Line writers' group, facilitates poetry groups and is on the Board of Directors, all at the Gloucester Writers Center, part of whose mission is "to encourage each other to write, speak, and learn about the world around us in order to participate in its transformation."

Moss on Stone and *Time and Tide* available on Amazon

mossonstone.author@gmail.com
mossonstoneauthor.blogspot.com
cosmicseanotes.blogspot.com